Waiting For Mom

Story by Linda Wagner Tyler
Pictures by Susan Davis

Puffin Books

PUFFIN BOOKS
Published by the Penguin Group
Viking Penguin, a division of Penguin Books USA Inc.,
40 West 23rd Street, New York, New York 10010, U.S.A.
Penguin Books Ltd, 27 Wrights Lane, London W8 5TZ, England
Penguin Books Australia Ltd, Ringwood, Victoria, Australia
Penguin Books Canada Ltd, 2801 John Street, Markham, Ontario, Canada L3R 1B4
Penguin Books (N.Z.) Ltd, 182–190 Wairau Road, Auckland 10, New Zealand

Penguin Books Ltd, Registered Offices; Harmondsworth, Middlesex, England

First published in the United States of America by Viking Penguin,
a division of Penguin Books USA Inc., 1987
Published in Picture Puffins 1989
1   3   5   7   9   10   8   6   4   2
Text copyright © Linda Wagner Tyler, 1987
Illustrations copyright © Susan Davis, 1987
All rights reserved

LIBRARY OF CONGRESS CATALOGING-IN-PUBLICATION DATA
Tyler, Linda Wagner.
Waiting for mom / story by Linda Wagner Tyler :
pictures by Susan Davis.   p.   cm.
"First published in the United States of America by Viking Penguin Inc., 1987"—T.p. verso.
Summary: A young hippo is worried and concerned when his mother,
caught up in an unexpected delay, is late picking him up from school.
ISBN 0 14 050652 7
[1. Mothers and sons—Fiction.   2. Hippopotamus—Fiction.]
I. Davis, Susan, 1948– ill.   II. Title.
PZ7.T94Wai 1989   [E]—dc19   89-30223

Printed in Japan by Dai Nippon Printing Co. Ltd.
Set in Souvenir Light

There's the three o'clock bell—time to go home.

My friend Tucky always beats me down
the stairs.

His Mom was waiting. I watched them pull away.

I waved goodbye to Macey. She is lucky;
her Mom drives a big van.

I looked up and down the street.

I couldn't see my Mom's car anywhere.

After a while the after-school kids came out
to the playground. I wanted to play with them
but I knew my Mom wouldn't like it if
she drove up and I was not waiting.

Mr. Mitt, my gym teacher, came by
on his way home.
He told me I was welcome to join the
after-school kids when they went inside.

My teacher Mrs. O'Connell came out.
She was on her way home too. She was
surprised to see me still in front of school.

We talked about how there must be a good reason

for my Mom being so late.

I know Mom wouldn't ever forget me.

She teaches school in the morning and maybe
she had a real bad kid who had to stay
after school for a long time.

I wonder if there was a fire at my Mom's school
and she was still helping children to escape.
It would be like her to do that.

We went to Mrs. Branch's office.

She is the principal of the whole school.

Mrs. Branch called my Mom's school.

They said she had left almost an hour ago.

I heard a car door outside and ran to the window
to see if it was my Mom.

It was only a delivery truck filled with milk.

Now I know how we get our milk for lunch.

One of the seventh-graders came in to do some
work for Mrs. Branch on the computer. He showed
me which keys to press so I could help too.

Then I went with Ms. Ling, the art teacher, to
unpack new supplies. I helped her roll new clay
into balls. That was really fun.

Mrs. O'Connell and Mrs. Branch decided I should
sit at the top of the front steps. Mrs. Branch
was going to stay in her office. I ate the broken
pieces of cookie in the bottom of my lunch box.

I watched the hands of the clock on the church
steeple. They moved so slowly.

I saw two red cars go by but neither one
was my Mommy's.

Then I heard a loud horn blowing down the street.

It was the horn on my Mom's car.

She was honking like crazy!

She flew out of the car and I ran down the stairs.

She gave me the biggest hug ever and I gave her
one right back.

She told me what had happened and why she couldn't get to a phone. It was scary for her too.

And I showed her where the after-school kids
play, in case it ever happens again.

On the way home we were so hungry that Mom
stopped to buy us a great big pizza.

Mom said she was so proud of me for being brave.

I told her she was a pretty brave Mommy too.